This book belongs to:

A Fishing Surprise

by Rae A. McDonald

illustrated by Kathleen Kemly

NorthWord
Minnetonka, Minnesota

The illustrations were created using watercolor, pastels, and pastel pencil
The text and display type were set in Litterbox ICG and ITC Usherwood
Composed in the United States of America
Art directed and designed by Lois A. Rainwater
Edited by Kristen McCurry

NorthWord
Books for Young Readers

11571 K-Tel Drive
Minnetonka, MN 55343
www.tnkidsbooks.com

Library of Congress Cataloging-in-Publication Data

McDonald, Rae A.
A fishing surprise / by Rae A. McDonald ; illustrated by Kathleen Kemly.
p. cm.
Summary: A sister and brother go fishing, but come home with a net full of apples instead.
ISBN 978-1-55971-977-3 (hardcover)
[1. Fishing--Fiction. 2. Apples--Fiction. 3. Brothers and sisters--Fiction.
4. Stories in rhyme.] I. Kemly, Kathleen, ill. II. Title.

PZ8.3.M14635Fi 2007
[E]--dc22   2007001156

Printed in Singapore
10 9 8 7 6 5 4 3 2 1

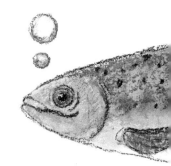

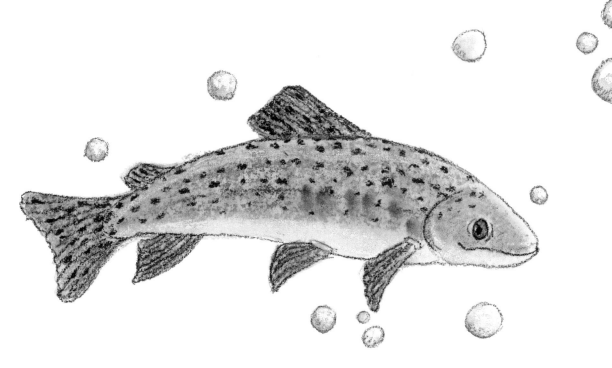

To Frederick and Hillary, the apples of my eye
—R.A.M.

For my guys—Brian, Adam and Chris
—K.K.

The author wishes to extend thanks to
Kristen McCurry for plucking this apple from the barrel.

Sunny day
Laze and play
Toss the line
It's fishing time!

Worms a-wiggling

Lots of giggling

Holding tight

Bobbers in sight...

We're hungry
We're hungry
for fish tonight!

Out of view

Breezes blew

Apples dropped

Plip kerplop

Slish and slosh
Apples wash
Appily quackily
Bobbling happily

Spin and swirl

Fish twirl

Biddily bop

Frogs hop

Stream hushes

In the rushes

Heron wades

Apples parade

Eyes on the water

Sun feeling hotter

Sitting fishing

Mostly wishing...

Still hungry
Still hungry
For fish tonight!

Suddenly
Look and see!
What's that floating?
Apples boating!

Hurry, scurry
What a flurry!
Follow the trail
Fill up the pail

Nets dip
Apples flip
Water dripping
Feet a-slipping

Nets so full

Buckets to pull

Rest awhile

Walked a mile

Overhead

Green and red

Tree, it was you!
Thank yoodle-dee-doo!

Fishing done
Time to run
Ho hey!
What'll they say?

Did you catch
any fish today?

We'll sing and shout
And haul our catch out
We'll yell surprise!
No fish to fry!
We're hungry
We're hungry
for apple pie!

RAE A. MCDONALD has always made her home by water—from the little lake of her Minnesota childhood to the great Puget Sound near her western Washington home today. Rae has been a school librarian for 25 years but always finds time for her other passions—the outdoors and the arts. She "fishes" for new story ideas when gardening, biking, and working with her students. *A Fishing Surprise* is Rae's first picture book.

KATHLEEN KEMLY grew up in Michigan and moved to New York to study art at Parsons School of Design. After working in toy packaging for a few years, she and her husband began moving west. They eventually landed in Seattle where they now live with their two sons, two cats, two chickens, and a guinea pig. In addition to painting and exhibiting, Kathleen also works with children as an artist in residence for middle school students.